CINDERELLA
THE SEQUEL

When the fairy tale ends and real life begins.

AMY LEW AND BETTY LOU BETTNER

Designed and Illustrated by
CATHY BENNETT

Copyright© 1995 by Amy Lew and Betty Lou Bettner. All rights reserved. Printed in Canada. No part of this book may be used or reproduced in any manner whatsoever without written permission.

Illustrations © 1997 by Cathy Bennett.

ISBN 0-9624841-9-9
Library of Congress Card Catalogue No. 97-66115

Connexions Press books are available from

Connexions Press, 10 Langley Road, Suite 200, Newton Centre, MA 02159
Telephone: 617 332-3220, Fax: 617 332-7863

and from

Connexions Press, 1 Old State Road, Media, PA 19063
Telephone/Fax: 610 566-1004

The ideal relationship produces "...*the feeling that you are worthwhile, that you cannot be replaced, that your partner needs you, that you are acting well, and that you are a fellow [hu]man and a true friend.*"
Alfred Adler, M.D.

This is dedicated to our children, their children, and the people they love.

Sarah, Kate, Mark, Michelle, Matthew, and Todd. May your relationships be nourishing, respectful, loving, and fun.

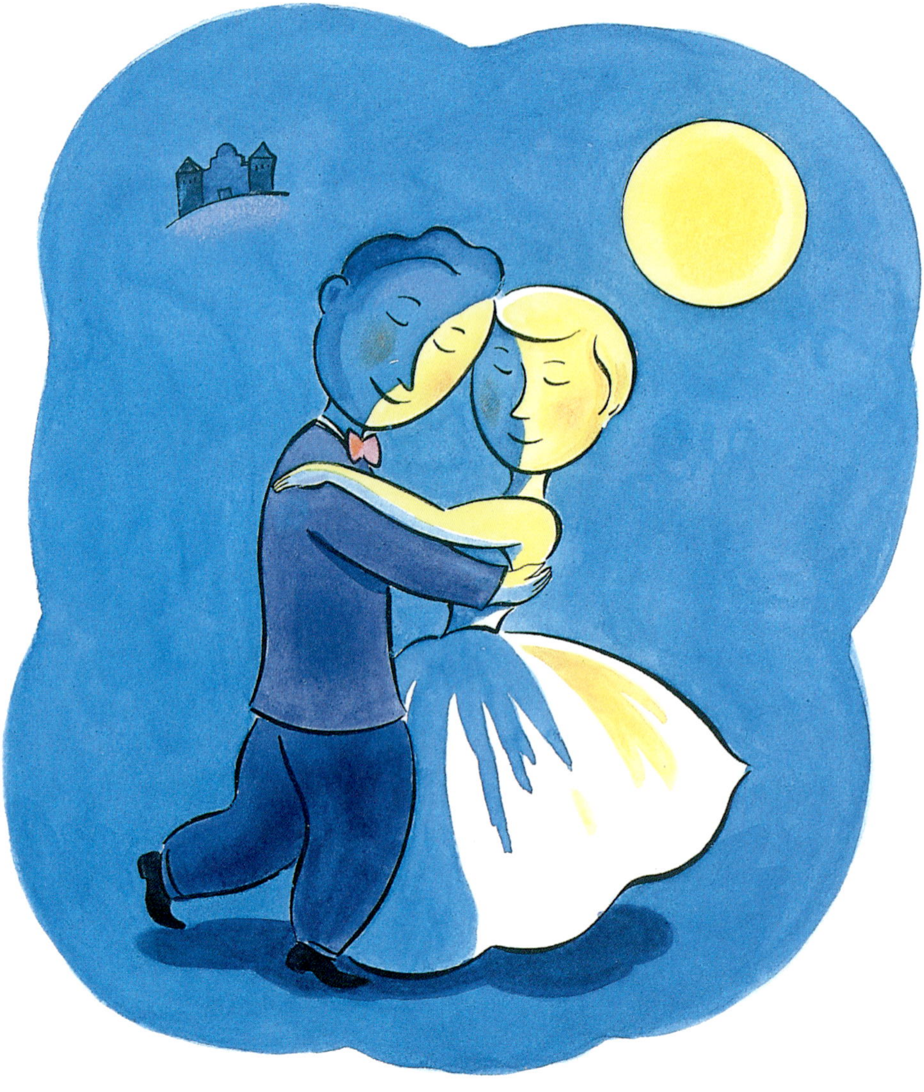

Most people are familiar with the story of Prince Charming and Cinderella, how they met and fell in love, lost each other, found each other, and danced off into the sunset. But as with most fairy tales, the story ended just when the real work began. Let's take a closer look at these two people and at what probably happened after they got married and set up housekeeping in the palace.

Prince Charming was the only child of doting parents and the darling of the whole kingdom. He was spoiled and pampered by all, as long as he followed palace protocol, behaved in a "princely" manner, and did what his parents wished.

The time had come for him to marry and he was looking for the perfect wife (someone who would indulge him without all the conditions that his parents placed on him). His only problem was, all the women he met were princesses and they were looking for the same thing. They too expected to be doted on, not to *do* the doting.

The Prince had just about given up hope of ever finding someone who was both "princess-like" and admiring when he saw Cinderella for the first time at the ball. She was dressed as a princess, a woman worthy of his attention, and yet, she didn't act like other princesses he had known. She didn't expect special treatment, she was happy just to have his attention. When they danced she looked at him with stars in her eyes and appreciated everything he said and did.

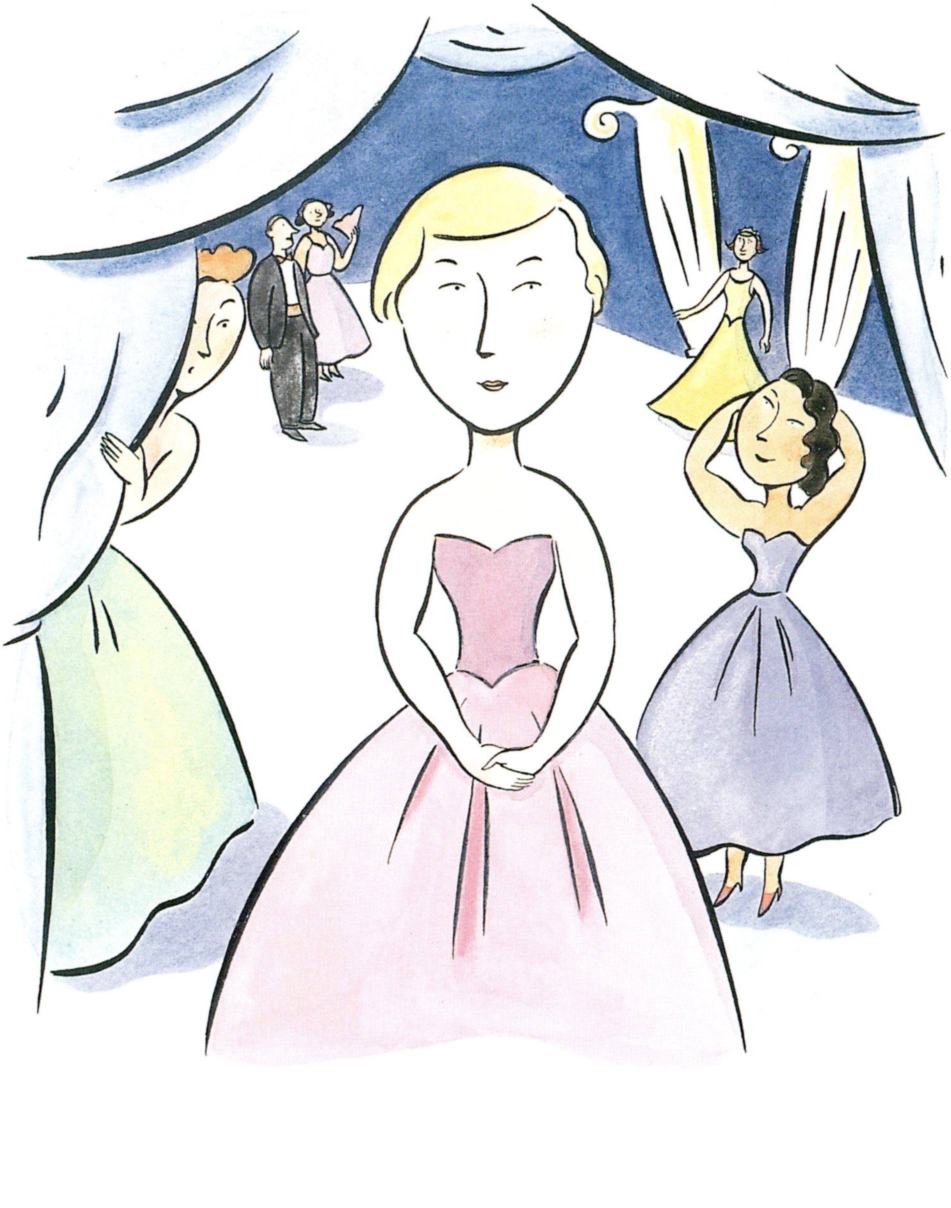

Cinderella started out as an only child with a loving and capable mother (who took total care of her family), but that blissful time ended when her mother died.

After her mother's death Cinderella's father felt unprepared to raise a daughter by himself and decided to remarry to get the help he needed. He found a woman with daughters of her own, who he thought would take care of things. She not only took care, *she took over*! Later, when Cinderella's father died, she felt abandoned and vulnerable. She was now left with a stepmother who she felt was cold and demanding and with her angry, critical stepsisters.

Cinderella's overwhelmed stepmother resented finding herself a single mom again, with yet another child to feed and clothe. She took her anger out on her stepdaughter who, as the tale goes, was only kept around for the work she could do. Cinderella felt uncared for and unwanted. Now she was an orphaned stepchild in the quintessential "dysfunctional family."

Imagine her delight when she arrived at the ball and was greeted by the handsome prince. Instead of her usual treatment she was treated with respect and consideration. The match seemed made in heaven and Cinderella and Prince Charming were soon married.

Everything went well until they returned to the castle after the honeymoon. Prince went upstairs to the bedroom and changed into his night clothes, leaving his shirt on the floor, his socks on the bed, and his pants on the chair. Cinderella came into the room and was shocked by the mess.

She waited, expectantly, for the prince to clean up, but when he didn't, she began to drop some hints. When he didn't respond, the hints got stronger and a familiar thought entered her mind. "Aha, he's just like all the others. I thought he was different, but he expects me to clean up his mess too. He just wants a servant."

Pretty soon Cinderella was feeling uncared for and unwanted again. Instead of asking the Prince why he wasn't picking up his clothes she jumped to her next conclusion — "He doesn't love me!"

Meantime the Prince couldn't figure out what had happened to his attentive and adoring bride. "All she seems to do is pick, pick, pick. She's always expecting more of me. She couldn't really be that upset about a little mess. She's just like all the others," he concluded, "she's trying to *make* me do what she wants."

Instead of sitting down and talking to each other about their feelings, their beliefs about their roles in the marriage, and their expectations of each other, they both jumped to another mistaken conclusion. "When I met my perfect mate I was supposed to live happily ever after. I'm not happy; therefore, you must not be the perfect mate."

At this point, Cinderella and the Prince decided that they should give a call to Merlina, the marriage counselor. Both of them were convinced that the other was at fault. If only Merlina could magically make the other person change, everything would be okay. But Merlina was a marriage counselor, not a magician and, besides, her experience had taught her that just changing behaviors wouldn't get to the heart of the real issues.

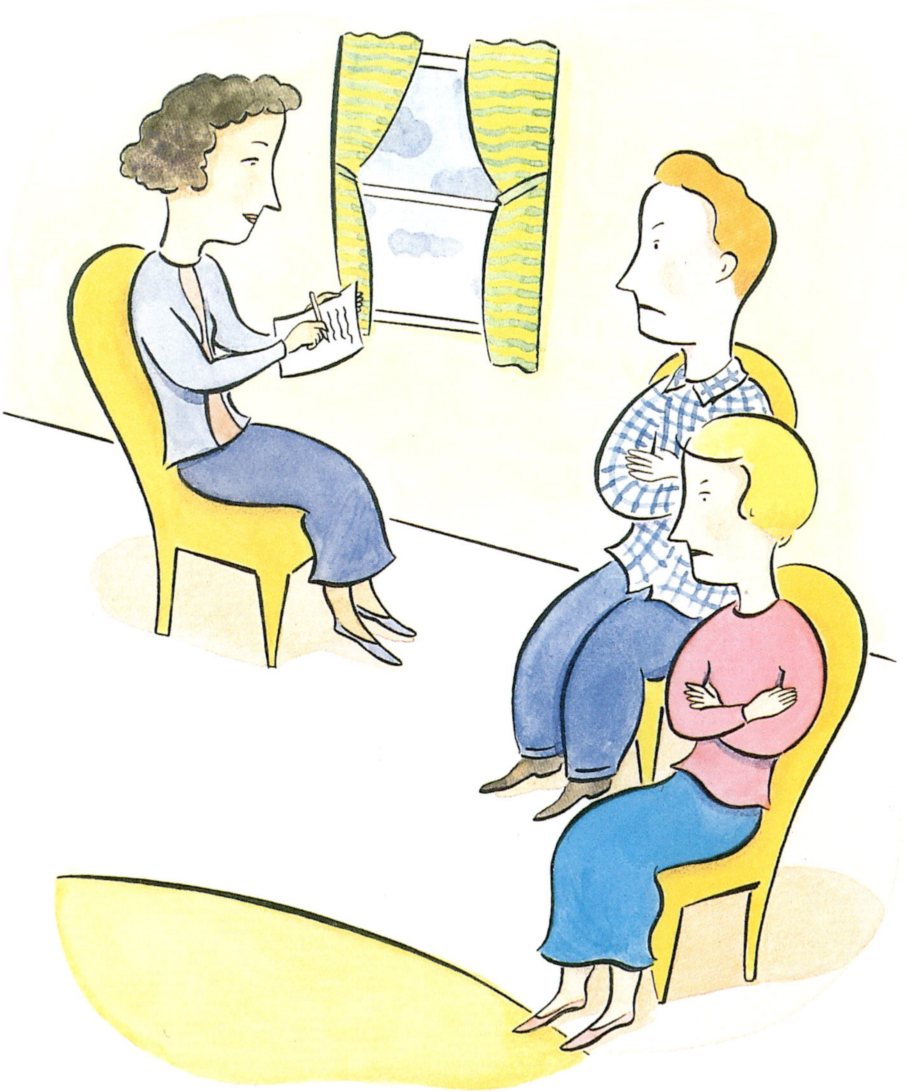

Merlina knew that both Cinderella and Prince Charming had entered their relationship with preconceived ideas about the meaning of behavior and expectations about what men and women should do. Their individual perspectives influenced how they interpreted each other's behavior.

Merlina helped them to understand the dynamics of their relationship and how their expectations from the past were influencing their behavior in the present. She suggested that they were attracted to each other for similar reasons — that both wanted to find someone who would make them feel as special as they had felt in early childhood.

The Prince had been delighted to find an "equal" who looked up to him, and Cinderella had been thrilled to find a "superior" who treated her like a princess (equal). While both *hoped* for special treatment, what they *expected* was the "conditional" treatment they had previously received. She expected to be taken advantage of and he expected someone to try to control him.

Now that each of them could see how the other was interpreting the situation, each could begin to understand the other's behavior. What each had previously seen as a sign that the other didn't care was really the other's attempt to be cared for.

The Prince told Cinderella, "I never expected you to clean up after me. That's what servants do. All I wanted was to have your uncritical love and affection."

A relieved Cinderella told the Prince, "I never wanted to make you do anything. I just didn't want you to treat me like a servant. I only wanted to be your partner."

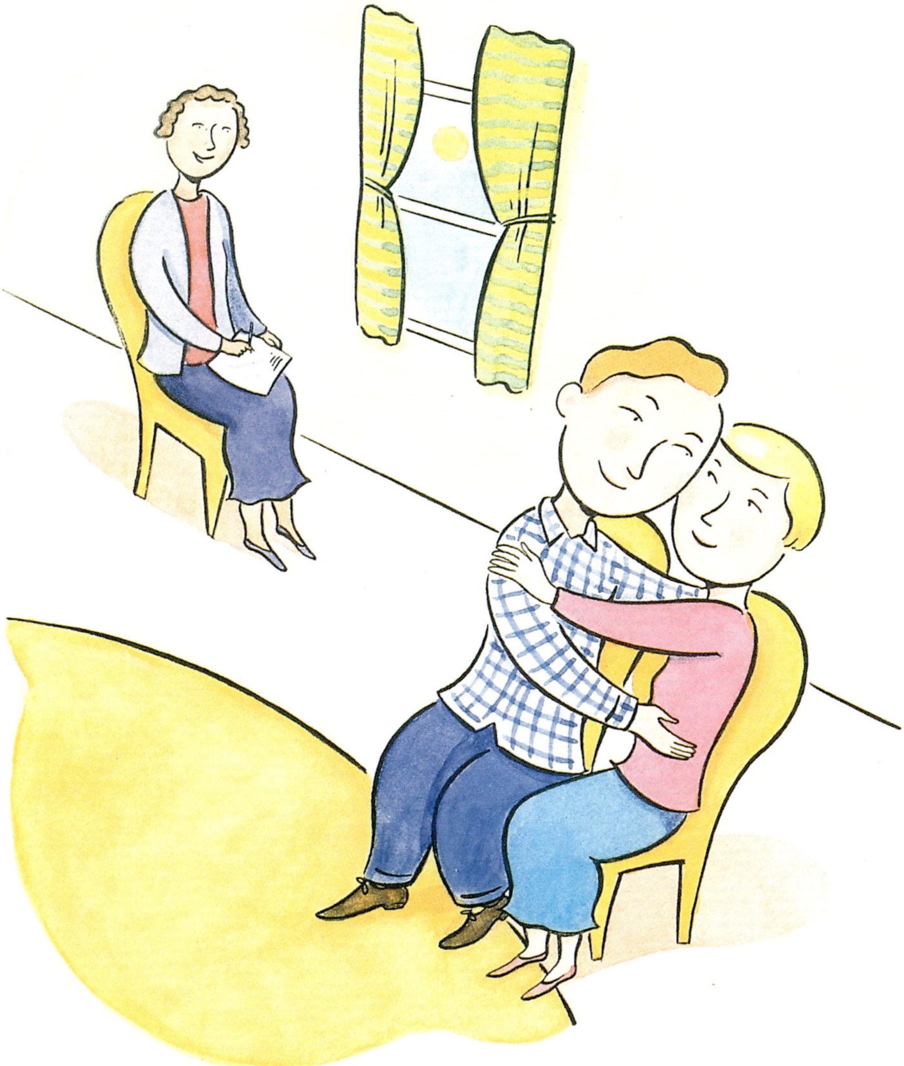

The happy couple felt so pleased and excited that they decided to celebrate. The Prince began to dream. "We'll have a great ball, and invite the whole kingdom."

At the same time Cinderella began to imagine a romantic getaway. "Just the two of us, no fuss, no bother."

Before they knew it, they were arguing again. "I knew it, you don't love me," said Cinderella. "You never want to spend time with me alone, you only want me to entertain your guests."

The Prince was angry too. He was just about to start his long list of complaints when he caught Merlina's eye. "Wait a minute," he said. "I do love you, and I'm so proud of you that I just wanted to show you off. I guess I just didn't stop to think about how you might feel about being in a huge gathering of my friends."

"And I should have asked you what you were thinking before I planned a trip," said Cinderella.

Merlina interrupted at this point. "Learning about each other's childhood and seeing things from each other's point of view is very helpful, but old habits die hard. Neither of you has had any experience with equal, respectful relationships. Remember there are no 'perfect' relationships, that only happens in fairy tales. In real life relationships take good will, commitment, and a willingness to learn from our mistakes."

Cinderella and Prince Charming knew in their hearts that Merlina was right. They decided that it would be a good idea to learn some effective communication techniques and have regular meetings to check out their perceptions and expectations.

They returned to the palace where they lived ....
ever after.

Merlina's Counseling Notes —*Cinderella and Prince Charming*

Today was the last session with Cindy and Prince. They seem to be putting the information they have learned about themselves to good use and are practicing the strategies they acquired in our sessions together.

It is clear that their early experiences developed into a way of interpreting and being in the world that influenced all of their subsequent behavior.* Prince Charming's experience of always having to live up to other people's standards led him to hope for someone who would appreciate him just the way he was, but his expectation was to find someone who would find fault and try to control him. Cinderella also dreamed of being appreciated but her expectation was to be exploited. When they met, it seemed that their wishes had been fulfilled; but, their unconscious expectations led them to misinterpret each other's actions. Instead of checking out their perceptions they reacted to what they "believed" they saw. Their behavior actually brought on the reaction that they already expected to find.

Recommendations:
1. Continue to have weekly couples meetings to check out their perceptions and expectations and make their plans for the week.
2. Make sure to set aside time together to nourish their relationship and maintain intimacy; e.g., a cup of coffee, a walk, a regular date night. Have fun together.
3. Be sure to notice and acknowledge each other's strengths (they could incorporate this into their couple meeting).

*This concept, known as "life-style," was first described in 1929 by psychiatrist Alfred Adler, the founder of Individual Psychology.

The Crucial "Cs" of Intimacy

1. **Connectedness.** Each partner has the feeling of being **connected** to the other. This sense of belonging provides security and a belief that one's mate is dependable. People who feel connected are more likely to cooperate. Those who are unsure of their connection may complain that their partner doesn't pay enough attention to them.

2. **Capability.** Both partners feel **capable.** The knowledge that both partners can act independently enables them to "depend" upon each other without becoming "dependent". People who feel competent are self-reliant and more likely to assume and share responsibility. Those who are unsure of their competence may end up in frequent power struggles to compensate for feeling inadequate.

3. **Counting.** Both partners feel valued. Partners must feel like they **count** with each other, that their opinions and actions matter, and that what they do makes a positive difference. People who know they count are more likely to make a contribution. Those who don't feel that they matter may feel hurt and may try to hurt others to show them how it feels.

4. **Courage.** Both partners develop the **courage** necessary to learn about themselves, take responsibility for their own behavior, and work on the relationship. People who have courage are resilient and are able to enjoy good times and weather difficult times. Those who are discouraged feel hopeless, avoid difficult situations, and give up easily.

The Crucial "Cs" in Your Relationship

When do you feel a connection with your partner? When does your partner feel connected? How do you know? How do you help?

When do you feel capable in your relationship? When does your partner feel capable? How do you know? How do you help?

How do you know you count with your partner? When does your partner feel valued by you? How do you know? How do you help?

When do you feel encouraged? How do you encourage your partner?

Other books by these authors published by Connexions Press:

Raising Kids Who Can (1989, 1992, 1996)
Raising Kids Who Can: A Leader's Guide (1996)
Responsibility in the Classroom: A Teacher's Guide to Understanding
 and Motivating Students (1995)
A Parent's Guide to Understanding and Motivating Children (1996)

Connexions Press books are available from

Connexions Press, 10 Langley Road, Suite 200, Newton Centre, MA 02159
Telephone: 617 332-3220, Fax: 617 332-7863

and from

Connexions Press, 1 Old State Road, Media, PA 19063
Telephone/Fax: 610 566-1004

RELATIONSHIPS

Most people are familiar with the story of Prince Charming and Cinderella —how they met and fell in love, lost each other, found each other, and danced off into the sunset. But, as with most fairy tales, the story ends just when the real work begins. *Cinderella, the Sequel*, a charming fairy tale for adults, takes a closer look at these two people and what may have happened after they got married and set up housekeeping in the palace.

Amy Lew, Ph.D., and Betty Lou Bettner, Ph.D., are internationally recognized Adlerian family therapists. They have helped couples and individuals work on their relationships for over twenty years. Their concrete, light-hearted, and easy-to-use approach for understanding behavior has made their lectures and books popular with couples, parents, and teachers around the world. Their commitment to strengthening all relationships is further reflected in their *Raising Kids Who Can* series of books for parents and teachers.

Amy Lew, Ph.D   Betty Lou Bettner, Ph.D.

Connexions Press
Amy Lew photograph ©1996 by Ingrid
Betty Lou Bettner photograph ©1996 by Kathy Madison

Price: $12.00

CINDERELLA
THE SEQUEL

When the fairy tale ends and real life begins.

AMY LEW AND BETTY LOU BETTNER